The Phillie Phanatic's
MOVING DAY
by Tom Burgoyne
Illustrated by Len Epstein
Middle Atlantic Press

High atop *Veterans Stadium*, in his room behind the huge video scoreboard, the Phillie Phanatic was busy packing his clothes and favorite things into big cardboard boxes.

His favorite baseball team, the Phillies, was moving into a new ballpark
and the Phanatic was going with them.

"Mom, why do we have to move? I love our home now, the way it is," the Phanatic said. His mom Phoebe replied, "Don't worry, Phanatic, you are going to love your new home. Besides, you can bring all of your things along with you."

"But will I have my own room with my own bed and everything?" asked the Phanatic.
"Relax, Phanatic," Phoebe said. "The moving company will be here soon to make sure that your bed and all your things make it to the new ballpark."
"Even my lucky baseball glove?" asked the Phanatic.
"Yes. Phanatic," Phoebe sighed, "even your lucky baseball glove."

The Phillie Phanatic was excited to have a new place to call home, but he was also a little nervous. What will the new ballpark look like? Will he have fun there? Will he see his friends as much after he moves into his new home? Where will his room be? Where will he keep his lucky glove and his baseball card collection?

He decided to take a walk around the stadium to talk to some of his friends about all the questions he had.

The Phanatic went to visit his best friend Lefty. Lefty was a white cat with a black left paw who roamed around the stadium with some of his friends.

"Hey, be careful with that bed!" Lefty called out to one of the movers. "I'm going to need that in my new home."

"Lefty, are you moving to the new ballpark, too?" the Phillie Phanatic asked.
"You betcha, Phanatic. I wouldn't miss it for the world!"
"Are you going to have your own room?" the Phanatic asked.
"Nah, I'll probably be stuck in a broom closet or out by the trash dumpster," Lefty moaned.

The Phanatic continued to walk around the stadium. He spotted Bruce the Vendor busy packing, too.
"Hi, Bruce," called the Phanatic. "Are you moving to the new ballpark, too?"
"Yes, I am, Phanatic," said Bruce. "There is a lot of work to be done. I've got to make sure that the new ballpark has plenty of hot dogs, popcorn, soda and other goodies."

The Phillie Phanatic was excited. He loved eating food during the baseball game. He helped Bruce shovel popcorn onto the back of his truck. He was happy that Bruce was moving to the new ballpark and that all his favorite foods would be there, too.

Next, the Phanatic saw his friend Froggy busy working on the baseball field. Froggy was a member of the ground crew. It was the ground crew's job to take care of the field. "What are you doing, Froggy?" asked the Phillie Phanatic.

"The movers come today, Phanatic, and I've got to make sure that all of the bases make it over to the new ballpark," Froggy said.
"You mean you're moving, too?" the Phanatic asked.
"Sure, Phanatic! I can't wait to see our new home!" Froggy exclaimed.

The Phanatic helped Froggy pack the bases into a big brown box so that the movers could take them over to the new ballpark. After he finished helping Froggy, the Phanatic went back to his room to finish packing his things.

When the Phanatic opened the door to his room, he noticed that his bed and all of his things were gone! The walls where his posters hung were bare. The shelves where he kept his baseball cards were empty. Even his lucky baseball glove had disappeared!

Where had all his things gone, the Phanatic wondered. He rushed out of his room and hopped on his trusty four-wheeler. The Phanatic drives his red four-wheeler at all the Phillies games and now he was going to use it to find his belongings.

Up ahead he saw a moving van. Where was that big moving van going? Maybe it was going to the new ballpark. The Phanatic followed close behind. Maybe that van would lead him to all of his things.

Then the Phanatic saw it – his new home – Citizens Bank Park! It was beautiful!
It was made of bricks and red steel and it had lights stretching up to the sky.

It was different than his old home but the Phanatic liked it! The moving van drove right up to the new ballpark and down a big ramp. The Phanatic followed close behind.

The Phanatic searched the ballpark for his belongings.
He looked in the new locker room, but his things weren't there.

He looked for his things in the new Phillies dugout, but his things weren't there either.

He looked over by the new food stand and saw his friend Bruce the Vendor. "Hi, Phanatic!" Bruce shouted out. "Isn't our new home great? I have a new popcorn popper, a new refrigerator and a brand new grill to cook all of the hot dogs!"

Next, he saw his pal Froggy.
"Hey, Phanatic," called Froggy, "Look, I have a new lawn mower to help me take care of our brand new baseball field. Yippee!"

The Phanatic was happy that his friends loved their new home but he couldn't stop to talk.
He was busy trying to find out where all his things had gone.

Just then, he saw his friend Lefty. "Phanatic, have you seen my bed?" asked the white cat with the black left paw. "I looked for it by the trash dumpster and in all of the broom closets, but I can't find it anywhere."

"Come with me, Lefty," the Phanatic said to his friend.
"Maybe we can find our things together."

After walking all around the new park, the Phillie Phanatic and Lefty came to a big door with a red star painted on it. "Maybe my things are in here, Lefty," said the Phanatic.

When they opened the door, they saw all of the Phillie Phanatic's things neatly put away in their place. His pennants and posters were hanging on the walls and his baseball card collection was stacked in boxes on the shelves in the corner. Phoebe Phanatic was there, too.

"Are you looking for this, Phillie Phanatic?" Phoebe asked.
"My lucky baseball glove!" the Phanatic shouted.
Phoebe looked at the Phanatic and said to him, "I hope you don't mind, Phanatic, but I had the movers pack up all your belongings and put them in your new room."

"You mean this is my room?" asked the Phanatic.
"That's right, Phanatic," said Phoebe. "Welcome to your new home!"
"Thanks, Mom, but where is my bed?" the Phanatic asked.

“Follow me,” Phoebe replied. She led the Phanatic and Lefty to the Phanatic’s bedroom.

When they looked inside they saw the Phillie Phanatic's bed and right beside it there was a small bed for Lefty.

"Look, Lefty, you get to sleep in my room. I think we are going to love our new home!" said the Phanatic.
"And I know one thing, Phanatic," said Lefty.

"This sure beats the broom closet!" the little cat said.
And together they laughed into the night.